STO ✓

THE ARKANSAW BEAR

Frontispiece—*Arkansaw Bear.*

"'YOU CAN CALL ME RATIO, TOO, SEE?'"

See p. 25.

THE
ARKANSAW BEAR

A Tale of Fanciful Adventure

Told in Song and Story by
ALBERT BIGELOW PAINE

In Pictures by
FRANK VER BECK

HARPER & BROTHERS
NEW YORK AND LONDON

Copyright, 1898, by Robert Howard Russell.

Copyright, 1902, by Henry Altemus.

Copyright, 1925, by Albert Bigelow Paine.

D-T

The Arkansaw Bear. PRINTED IN THE
UNITED STATES OF AMERICA

Dedication

TO MASTER FRANK VER BECK,

FOR WHOSE

BEDTIME ENTERTAINMENT

THE ARKANSAW BEAR

FIRST PERFORMED

CONTENTS

CHAPTER		PAGE
I.	THE MEETING OF BOSEPHUS AND HORATIO	15
II.	THE FIRST PERFORMANCE	39
III.	HORATIO AND THE DOGS	57
IV.	THE DANCE OF THE FOREST PEOPLE	77
V.	GOOD-BYE TO ARKANSAW	95
VI.	AN EXCITING RACE	111
VII.	HORATIO'S MOONLIGHT ADVENTURE	133
VIII.	SWEET AND SOUR	153
IX.	IN JAIL AT LAST	175
X.	AN AFTERNOON'S FISHING	193
XI.	THE ROAD HOME	213
XII.	THE BEAR COLONY AT LAST. THE PARTING OF BOSEPHUS AND HORATIO	237

ILLUSTRATIONS

	PAGE
"'You can call me Ratio, too, see?'" . *Frontispiece.*	
"His blood turned cold"	19
"'Maybe you can play it yourself, eh?'"	23
"'We can play and sing as we go'"	33
"'Once more Bo, once more!'"	43
"'Run zigzag, Bo! and don't drop the melon'"	47
"In a second more he was playing and dancing"	51
"Horatio paused and listened"	63
"Bo made at them with his stick"	67
"Horatio sat astride a big limb"	71
"'Let's count the money, Bo'"	81
"Other friends slipped into the magic circle"	89
"He fell headlong into a clump of briars"	103
"The negroes patted and danced crazily"	108
"The little boy and the big Bear slept soundly"	115
"Horatio lay clawing the air wildly"	121
"'Horatio! Our money! It is gone!'"	125
"The fat fugitive leaped into the river"	129
"'These little darky babies are very—amusing'"	137

ILLUSTRATIONS

	PAGE
"Every little way he paused"	141
"Horatio was between him and the cabins"	145
"He bit it in half cheerfully"	161
"The Bear dashed past, striking at the swarm"	167
"His eyes and nose were swollen in great knots"	171
"'Is my hat becoming, Bo?'"	179
"'Shed them clothes or I'll shoot!'"	183
"Horatio on the bank was still shouting"	201
"'Hold on to the end of the log!'" shouted Bo	205
"'Sing, Horatio! It's your turn to sing!'"	209
"'Minda your own biz'"	219
"A half naked man was disappearing over the hill"	229
"'Right about! Ready! March!'"	233
"Bosephus at first enjoyed it immensely"	243
"The poor Bear wept on the little boy's shoulder"	247
"And they traveled on forever"	253

THE MEETING OF BOSEPHUS AND HORATIO

THE ARKANSAW BEAR

CHAPTER I

THE MEETING OF BOSEPHUS AND HORATIO

"Oh, 't was down in the woods of the Arkansaw,
And the night was cloudy and the wind was raw,

And he did n't have a bed and he did n't have a bite,
And if he had n't fiddled he'd 'a' traveled all night."

BOSEPHUS paused in his mad flight to listen. Surely this was someone playing the violin, and the tune was familiar. He listened more intently.

"But he came to a cabin and an old gray man,
And says he, 'Where am I going? Now tell
me if you can—'"

It was the "Arkansaw Traveler," and close at hand. The little boy tore hastily through the brush in the direction of the music. The moon had come up, and he could see quite well, but he did not pause to pick his way. As he stepped from the thicket out into an open space the fiddling ceased. It was bright moonlight there, too, and as Bosephus looked, his blood turned cold.

In the center of the open space was a large tree. Backed up against this tree, and looking straight at the little boy, with fiddle in position for playing and uplifted bow, was a huge Black Bear!

Bosephus looked at the Bear, and the Bear looked at Bosephus.

"Who are you, and what are you doing here?" he roared.

"I—I am Bo-se-Bosephus, an' I—I g-guess I'm l-lost!" gasped the little boy.

"HIS BLOOD TURNED COLD."

"Guess you are!" laughed the Bear, as he drew the bow across the strings.

"An-an' I have n't had any s-supper, either."

"Neither have I!" grinned the Bear, "that is, none worth mentioning. A young rabbit or two, perhaps, and a quart or so of blackberries, but nothing real good and strengthening to fill up on." Then he regarded Bosephus reflectively, and began singing as he played softly:—

"Oh, we'll have a little music first and then some supper, too,
But before we have the supper we will play the music through."

"No hurry, you know. Be cool, please, and don't wiggle so."

But Bosephus, or Bo, as he was called, was very much disturbed. He could see there was no prospect of supper for anybody but the Bear.

"You'll forget all about supper pretty soon," continued the Bear, fiddling.

"You'll forget about your supper—you'll forget about your home—
You'll forget you ever started out in Arkansaw to roam."

THE ARKANSAW BEAR

"My name is Horatio," he continued. "Called Ratio, for short. But I don't like it. Call me Horatio, in full, please."

"Oh, ye-yes, sir!" said Bo, hastily.

"See that you don't forget it!" grunted the Bear. "I don't like familiarity in my guests. But I am getting away from the song I was singing when you came tearing out of that thicket. Seems like I never saw anybody in such a hurry to see me as you were.

"Now the old man sat a-fiddling by the little cabin door,
   And the tune was pretty lively, and he played it o'er and o'er;
   And the stranger sat a-list'ning and a-wond'ring what to do,
   As he fiddled and he fiddled, but he never played it through."

Bo was very fond of music, and as Horatio drew from the strings the mellow strains of "The Arkansaw Traveler" he forgot that both he and the Bear were hungry. He could dance very well, and was just about to do so as the Bear paused.

"Why don't you play the rest of that tune, Horatio?" he asked, anxiously.

"Same reason the old man did n't!" growled the Bear, still humming the air,

"Oh, raddy-daddy dum—daddy dum—dum—
    dum—"

"Why!" continued Bo, "that's funny!"

"Is it?" snorted Horatio; "I never thought so!"

"Then the stranger asked the fiddler, 'Won't you
    play the rest for me?'
'Don't know it,' says the fiddler; 'Play it for
    yourself!' says he—"

"Maybe you can do what the stranger did, Bosephus—maybe you can play it yourself, eh?" grunted the huge animal, pausing and glowering at the little boy.

"Oh, no, sir—I—I—that is, sir, I can only wh-whistle or s-sing it!" trembled Bo.

"What!"

"Y-yes, sir. I—"

"'MAYBE YOU CAN PLAY IT YOURSELF, EH?'"

"You can sing it?" shouted the Bear, joyfully, and for once forgetting to fiddle. "You don't say so!"

"Why, of course!" laughed Bo; "everybody in Arkansaw can do that. It goes this way:—

"Then the stranger took the fiddle, with a ridy-
diddle-diddle,
And the strings began to jingle at the tingle of
the bow,

While the old man sat and listened, and his
eyes with pleasure glistened,
As he shouted 'Hallelujah! And hurray—for
—Joe!'"

When Bo had finished, Horatio stood perfectly still for some moments in astonishment and admiration. Then he came up close to the little boy.

"Look here, Bo," he said, "if you'll teach me to play and sing that tune, we'll forget all about that sort o' personal supper I was planning on, and I'll take you home all in one piece. And anything you want to know I'll tell you, and anything I've got, except the fiddle, is yours. Furthermore, you can call me Ratio, too, see?

'Oh, ridy-diddle-diddle—'

how does it go? Give me a start, please."

Bo brightened up at once. He liked to teach things immensely, and especially to ask questions.

"Why, of course, Ratio," he said, condescendingly; "I shall be most happy. And I can make up poetry, too. Ready, now:—

I am glad to be the teacher of this kind and
    gentle creature,
Who can play upon the fiddle in a—"

"Wait, Bo! wait till I catch up!" cried Horatio, excitedly. "Now!"

"Hold on, Ratio. I want to ask a question!"

"All right! Fire away! I could n't get any further anyhow."

THE ARKANSAW BEAR

"Well," said Bo, "I want to know how you ever learned to play the fiddle."

Horatio did not reply at first, but closed his eyes reflectively and drew the bow across the strings softly.

> "Oh, raddy-daddy dum—daddy dum—dum—dum—

"I took a course of lessons," he said, presently, "but it is a long story, and some of it is not pleasant. I think we had better go on with the music now:—

> "Oh, there was a little boy and his name was Bo,
> Went out into the woods when the moon was getting low,
> And he met an Old Bear who was hungry for a snack,
> And his folks are still awaiting for Bosephus to come back."

"Go right on with the rest of it," said Bo, hastily.

"For the boy became the teacher of this kind and
    gentle creature,
Who can play upon the fiddle in a very skilful
    way."

"But I say, Ratio," interrupted Bo again, "how did it come you never learned to play the second part of that tune?"

Horatio scowled fiercely at first, and then once more grew quite pensive. He played listlessly as he replied:—

"Ah," he said, "my teacher was—was unfortunate. He taught me to play the first part of that tune. He would have taught me the rest of it—if he had had time."

Horatio drew the bow lightly across the strings and began to sing, in a far-away voice:—

"Oh, there was an old man, and his name was
    Jim,
And he had a pet bear who was fond of
    him;

But the man was very cruel and abusive to his pet,
And one day his people missed him, and they have n't found him yet."

"Oh!" said Bo; "and w-what happened, Horatio?"

Horatio paused and dashed away a tear.

"It happened in a lonely place," he said, chewing thoughtfully, "a lonely place in the woods, like this. We were both of us tired and hungry, and he grew impatient and beat me. He also spoke of my parents with disrespect, and in the excitement that followed he died."

"Oh!" said Bo.

"Yes," repeated Horatio, "he died. He was such a nice man—such a nice, fat Italian man, and so good while—while he lasted."

"Oh!" said Bo.

Horatio sighed.

"His death quite took away my appetite," he mused. "I often miss him now, and long

THE ARKANSAW BEAR

for some one to take his place. I kept this fiddle, though, and he might have been teaching me the second part of that tune on it now if his people had n't missed him—that is, if he had n't been impatient, I mean."

"Oh, Ratio!" said Bo, "I will teach you the tune all through! And I will never be the least bit impatient or—or excited. Are you ready to begin, Ratio?"

"All ready! Play."

"Oh, it's fine to be the teacher of a kind and
    gentle creature
Who can play upon the fiddle in a very skilful
    way ;
And I 'll never, never grieve him, and I 'll
    never, never leave him,
Till I hear the rooster crowing for the break
    —of—day."

"That was very nice, Bo, very nice indeed!" exclaimed Horatio, as they finished. "Now, I am going to tell you a secret."

"Oh!" said Bo.

"I have a plan. It is to start a colony for the education and improvement of wild bears. But first I am going to travel and see the world. I have lived mostly with men and know a good deal of their taste—tastes, I mean—and have already traveled in some of the States. After my friend, the Italian, was gone, I tried to carry out his plans and conduct our business alone. But I could only play the first part of that tune, and the people would n't stand it. They drove me away with guns and clubs. So I came back to the woods to practice and learn the rest of that music. My gymnastics are better—watch me."

Horatio handed Bo his fiddle and began a most wonderful performance. He stood on his head, walked on his hands, danced on two feet, three feet, and all fours. Then he began and turned somersaults. Bo was delighted.

"It was n't because you could n't play and

perform well enough!" he cried, excitedly. "It was because you went alone, and they thought you were a crazy, wild bear. If I could go along with you we could travel together over the whole world and make a fortune. Then we could buy a big swamp and start your colony. What do you say, Ratio? I am a charity boy, and have no home now anyway! We can make a fortune and see the world!"

At first Ratio did not say anything. Then he seized Bo in his arms and hugged him till the boy thought his time had come. The Bear put him down and held him off at arm's length, joyously.

"Say," he shouted. "Why, I say that you are a boy after my own heart! We'll start at once! I'll take you to a place to-night where there are lots of blackberries and honey, and to-morrow we will set forth on our travels. Here's my hand as a pledge of safety as long as you keep your word. You mean to do so, don't you?"

"Oh, yes," said Bo.

"And now for camp. We can play and sing as we go."

As the little boy took Horatio's big paw he ceased to be even the least bit afraid. He had at last found a strong friend, and was going forth into the big world. He had never been so happy in his life before.

"All right, Ratio!" he shouted. "One, two, three, play!"

And Ratio gave the bow a long, joyous scrape across the strings, and thus they began their life together—Bosephus whistling and the Bear playing and singing with all his might the pleasing strains of "The Arkansaw Traveler":—

"Oh, there was a little boy and his name was Bo,
   Went out into the woods when the moon was
      getting low,
   And he had n't had his supper, and his way he
      did n't know,

"'WE CAN PLAY AND SING AS WE GO.'"

THE ARKANSAW BEAR

So he did n't have a bite to eat nor any place
 to go.
Then he heard the ridy-diddle of Horatio and
 his fiddle,
And his knees began to tremble as he saw him
 standing there;
Now they 'll never, never sever, and they 'll
 travel on forever—
Bosephus, and the fiddle, and the Old—Black—
 Bear."

THE FIRST PERFORMANCE

CHAPTER II

THE FIRST PERFORMANCE.

"Oh, 't was down in the woods of the Arkansaw
I met an Old Bear with a very nimble paw;

He could dance and he could fiddle at the only
tune he knew,
And he fiddled and he fiddled, but he never
played it through."

BO was awake first, and Horatio still lay sound asleep. As the boy paused, the Bear opened one eye sleepily and reached lazily toward his fiddle, but dropped asleep again before his paw touched it. They had found a very cosy place in a big heap of dry leaves under some spreading branches, and Horatio, though fond of music, was still more fond of his morning nap. Bosephus looked at him a moment and began singing again, in the same strain:—

> "Then there came a little boy who could whistle
>   all the tune,
>   And he whistled and he sang it by the rising
>   of the moon;
>   And he whistled and he whistled, and he sang
>   it o'er and o'er,
>   Till Horatio learned the music that he never
>   learned before."

The Bear opened the other eye, and once more reached for his fiddle. This time he got hold of it, but before his other paw touched the bow he was asleep again. Bo waited a moment. Then he suddenly began singing the other part of the tune:—

"Yes, he learned it all so neatly and he played
    it all so sweetly
That he fell in love completely with the boy
    without a home;

And he said, 'No matter whether it is dark or
    sunny weather,
We will travel on together till the cows—
    come—home.'"

Before Bosephus finished the first two lines of this strain Horatio was sitting up straight and fiddling for dear life.

"Once more, Bo, once more!" he shouted, as they finished.

They repeated the music, and Horatio turned two handsprings without stopping.

"Now," he said, "we will go forth and conquer the world."

"I could conquer some breakfast first," said Bo.

"Do you like roasting ears?"

"Oh, yes," said Bo.

"Well, I have an interest in a little patch near here—that is, I take an interest, I should say, and you can take part of mine, or one of your own, if you like. It really does n't make any difference which you do, just so you take it before the man that planted it gets up."

"Why," exclaimed the boy, as they came out into a little clearing, "that is old Zack Todd's field!"

"It is, is it? Well, how did old Zack Todd get it, I 'd like to know."

"Why—why, I don't know," answered Bo, puzzled.

"Of course not," said the Bear. "And now, Bosephus, let me tell you something. The bears owned that field long before old

Zack Todd was ever thought of. We're just renting it to him on shares. This is rent day. We don't need to wake Zack up. You get over the fence and hand me a few of

"'ONCE MORE. BO, ONCE MORE.'"

the best ears you can get quick and handy, and you might bring one of those watermelons I see in the corn there, and we'll find a quiet place that I know of, and have our breakfast."

Bo hopped lightly over the rail fence, and, gathering an armful of green corn, handed it to Horatio. Then he turned to select a melon.

"Has Zack Todd got a gun, Bosephus?" asked the Bear.

"Yes, sir-ee. The best gun in Arkansaw, and he's a dead shot with it."

"Oh, he is! Well, maybe you better not be quite so slow picking out that melon. Just take the first big one you see and come on."

"Why, Zack wouldn't care for us collecting rent, would he?"

"Well, I don't know. You see, some folks are peculiar that way. Zack might forget it was rent day, and a man with a bad memory and a good gun can't be trusted. Especially when he's a dead shot. There, that one will do. Never mind about leaving a receipt—we'll mail it to him."

Bo scrambled back over the fence with the melon, and hastened as fast as he could after Horatio, who was already moving across the clearing with his violin under one arm and the green ears under the other.

"Wait, Ratio," called the little boy. "This melon is heavy."

"Is that a long-range gun, Bo?" called back the Bear.

"Carries a mile and a half."

"Can't you move up a little faster, Bo? I'm afraid, after all, that melon is bigger than we needed."

The boy was fat and he panted after his huge companion.

Suddenly there was a sharp report, and Bosephus saw a little tuft of fur fly from one of his companion's ears. Horatio dodged frantically and dropped part of his corn.

"Run zigzag, Bo!" he called, "and don't drop the melon. Run zigzag. He can't hit you so well then," and Horatio himself began such a performance of running first one way and then the other that Bo was almost obliged to laugh in spite of their peril.

"Is this what you call conquering the world, Ratio?" he called. Then, as he followed the Bear's example, he caught a backward glimpse out of the corner of his eye.

"Oh, Ratio, the whole family is after us. Zack Todd, and old Mis' Todd, and Jim, and the girls."

"How many times does that gun shoot?"

"Only once without loading."

"Muzzle loader?"

"Yep," panted Bo. "Old style."

"Good! Hold on to that melon. We'll get to the woods yet."

But Horatio was mistaken, for just as they dashed into the edge of the timber, with the pursuers getting closer every moment, right in front of them was a high barbed-wire fence

"'RUN ZIGZAG, BO! AND DON'T DROP THE MELON.'"

which the Todd family had built around the clearing but a few days before. The Bear dropped his corn, and the boy, with some haste, put down the melon. They then turned. The Todd family was entering the woods—old Zack and the gun in front. He had loaded it, and was putting on the cap as he ran.

"What shall we do, Bo? what shall we do now?" groaned Horatio.

They were in a fix, sure enough. Their enemy was upon them, and in a moment more the deadly gun would be leveled. Suddenly a bright thought occurred to Bo.

"I know," he shouted; "dance, Horatio! dance!"

Horatio still had his fiddle under his arm. He threw it into position and ran the bow over the strings. In a second more he was playing and dancing, and Bo was singing as though it were a matter of life and death, which, perhaps, it was:—

THE ARKANSAW BEAR

"Oh, there was a fine man and a mighty fine gun
And a Bear that played the fiddle and a boy that could n't run,

And the boy was named Bosephus and Horatio was the Bear,
And they could n't find a bite to eat for breakfast anywhere."

The Todd family stood still at this unexpected performance and stared at the two musicians. Old man Todd leaned his gun against a tree.

"Now they could n't buy their breakfast for their money all was spent,
So they dropped into a cornfield to collect a little rent;

"IN A SECOND MORE HE WAS PLAYING AND DANCING."

But they only took a melon and an ear of corn
or so,
And were going off to eat them where the butter
blossoms grow."

The Todd family were falling into the swing of the music. Old Mis' Todd and the girls were swaying back and forth and the men were beating time with their feet. Suddenly Bosephus changed to the second part of the tune.

"But the old man got up early with a temper
rather surly,
And he chased them with his rifle and to catch
them he was bound;

Till he heard the ridy-diddle of Horatio and
his fiddle,
Then he shouted, 'Hallelujah, girls, and all—
hands—'round!'"

THE ARKANSAW BEAR

The first line of this had started the Todd family. Old Zack swung old Mis' Todd, and Jim swung the girls. Then all joined hands and circled to the left. They circled around Bosephus and Horatio, who kept on with the music, faster and faster. Then there was a grand right and left and balance all—every one for himself—until they were breathless and could dance no more. Horatio stopped fiddling and when old man Todd could catch his breath he said to Bo:—

"Look a-here; that Bear of yours is a whole show by himself, and you 're another. Anybody that can play and sing like that can have anything I 've got. There 's my house and there 's my cornfield; help yourselves."

Bo thanked him and said that the corn and the melon already selected would do for the time. To please them, however, he would take up a modest collection. He passed his hat and received a silver twenty-five cent piece, a spool of thread with a needle in it, a one-bladed jack-knife, and two candy hearts with mottoes on them—the last being from the girls, who blushed and giggled as they dropped them in. Then he said good-by, and the Todd family showed them a gate that led into the thick woods. As the friends passed out of sight and hearing Bosephus paused and waved his handkerchief to the girls. A little later Horatio turned to him and said, gravely:

"That is what I call conquering the world, Bosephus. We began a little sooner and more abruptly than I had expected, but it was not badly done, and, all things considered, you did your part very well, Bosephus; very well indeed."

HORATIO AND THE DOGS

CHAPTER III

HORATIO AND THE DOGS

"Blossom on the bough and bird on the limb—
Old Black Bear sits a-grinning at him;

Sawing on his fiddle and a-grinning at the jay—
Grinning as he saws the only tune that he can play."

HORATIO leaned back against the tree and played lazily. Bosephus lay stretched full length on the leaves, following idly with any words that happened to fit the strain. A blue jay just over their heads bobbed up and down on a limber branch, waiting for them to go. The Bear took up the song as the boy paused:—

"Boy on the bank and bird on the tree—
Bird keeps a-bobbing and a-blinking at me;
Bobbing and a-blinking, and a-waiting for a bite—
Has n't had a thing to eat since late—last—night."

"I say, Ratio," interrupted Bo. "Suppose we move on and give Mr. Jay Bird a chance?"

Horatio grunted and rose heavily. After their adventure with the Todd family they had come to a pleasant spot in the woods by a clear stream of water. Bo, who had some matches in his pocket, had kindled a fire and roasted some of the corn, much to the disgust of Horatio, who did not like fire, and asked him why he did not roast the watermelon, too, while he was about it. Then they had eaten their breakfast together and taken a brief rest before setting forth again on their travels. A jay bird was waiting to peck the gnawed ears and melon rinds. He stared at the strange pair as they strolled away through the trees, the Bear still playing his favorite melody.

"Ratio," said Bo, pausing suddenly, "what is that I hear scurrying through the bushes every now and then?"

"Friends of mine, likely."

"Friends? What friends?"

"Oh, everything 'most. Wild cats, wolves, foxes, and a few wild bears, maybe."

"Wild cats! Bears! Wolves!"

"Why, yes. Often when I play in the moonlight they come out and dance for me."

"Oh!" said Bo.

"I have them all dancing together, sometimes. I'll have them dance for you before long."

"Oh, Ratio, will you?"

"Yes. It's a lot of fun, but there's no money

in it, and that's what we're after now, Bo. We're going to buy that swamp, you remember, and start that bear colony."

Bosephus was about to reply when Horatio paused and listened. There was the distant sound of dogs barking.

"Hello!" said Bo. We're coming to somewhere. Now we'll give our first regular performance. Come on, Ratio!"

Horatio hesitated.

"How many dogs do you suppose there are, Bo?" he asked, anxiously.

"About a dozen, I should think, big and little."

"Little dogs, Bo? Little yapping, snapping dogs?"

"That's what it sounds like, and some hounds and a big dog or two. You don't mind dogs, do you?"

"Oh, no, not in the least; but it's most too soon after breakfast to give a performance,

"HORATIO PAUSED AND LISTENED."

and, besides, all that noise would spoil the music."

But the little boy, who still had in his pocket the two candy hearts that had been given to him by the Todd girls, walked ahead proudly.

"You trust to me!" he said, flourishing a large stick. "I'll stop their noise pretty quick. I'm not afraid of dogs!"

The Bear followed some steps behind, looking ahead warily.

"I'm not afraid, either, you know," he said, anxiously. "Only when there are so many of them they get me mixed up on my notes, and one of them once had the ill manners to nip quite a piece out of my left hind leg."

Presently they came into an open space and plump upon a little cross-roads village. A gang of dogs gamboled upon the common, chasing stray geese and barking loudly. **Horatio paused.**

"Come back, Bo," he whispered. "There's no money in that crowd."

But Bosephus was already some distance ahead, stick in hand, and the dogs had spied him. They ceased barking for a moment, and two or three of the larger ones ran away. Then the little dogs began yelping again and came on in a swarm. Bo made at them with his stick, but they dodged past him, and in a moment more were circling and snapping around Horatio, who was waving his violin wildly with one paw and slapping like a man killing mosquitoes with the other.

"Quick, Bo!" he shouted. "Quick! Help! Murder!"

The little boy wanted to laugh, but ran up instead and began striking among the bevy of dogs that were torturing his friend. Some of them howled and ran off a few paces. Then they came flocking back. Suddenly Horatio thrust his violin into Bo's hand and ran swiftly

"BO MADE AT THEM WITH HIS STICK."

toward a large tree a few yards distant. The curs followed and jumped high into the air after him as he scrambled up to the lower limbs.

Bosephus hurried after them and struck at them so fiercely with his club that they ran yelping away. A number of villagers, attracted by the commotion, were now appearing from all quarters.

"Here come the people, Ratio," said Bo, grinning. "Now we can perform."

"All right, Bo," whispered the Bear, "but if you'll kindly hand me up that fiddle I believe I'll perform right where I am."

The boy passed up the violin and the Bear struck a few notes. By this time the people had collected. There was a blacksmith with a leather apron, and a painter with all colors of paint on his clothes. Behind them there came a woman with dough on her hands and another carrying a baby. Other men and women followed in the procession, and a dozen or so children of all ages. They halted a little way from the tree and stood staring. Horatio sat astride a big limb and commenced playing. Suddenly the boy threw back his head and began to sing:—

> "Oh, the dogs barked loud and the dogs barked low
> At an Old Black Bear and a boy named Bo.
> And the boy stood still and the Bear climbed the tree,
> While the people came a-running to see what they could see."

The children drew up close at the first line and held their breath to listen. As the boy paused they shouted and screamed with laughter at the sight of Horatio fiddling in the forks of the tree. The dogs sat in a row and howled plaintively.

"Sing some more," cried the woman with the baby; "it amuses my little Joey."

"HORATIO SAT ASTRIDE A BIG LIMB."

"Yes, the people came to see them, and the dogs they ran away,
And the boy began to sing and the Bear began to play,
Till it tickled all the children and it made the baby crow,
And it set the people dancing till they jumped —Jim—Crow."

"More! more!" shouted the people as they formed into cotillions and reels. "Sing us some more!"

"Oh, the ridy-diddle-diddle of Horatio and his fiddle,
And the singing of Bosephus they had never heard before;

And it set them all to spinning, and the music was so winning
That they wined them and they dined them until half-past four!"

THE ARKANSAW BEAR

"Wait! wait!" called the woman with the baby under her arm, "I'm all out of breath."

"No, no!" shouted the children and all the others. "Go on! Go on!"

So once more and yet another time the happy musicians repeated their performance, and then Bo politely passed his hat to the dancers. When he had been to each one his hat was heavy with many useful articles and *some* money.

"Bring your Bear down out of the tree," said the blacksmith, "and we will give you a feast on the common."

Bo beckoned to Horatio to climb down, but the big fellow hesitated.

The thought of a feast, however, was too much for him.

That night, when they had both danced again for the people and Horatio had given them an acrobatic exhibition, they strolled away through the evening loaded down with luxuries of all kinds. The villagers went with them to the outskirts, and called good luck after them. As they passed into the quiet shadows of the forest they once more heard the barking of dogs in the distance behind them.

"We have had a good day, Bosephus," said Horatio, with a long sigh of satisfaction. "We are on the road to fortune. To be sure, there are little thorns along the way—"

"Dogs, for instance—and guns."

"Trifles, Bosephus; trifles. Don't give them a second thought. Of course you are only a little boy as yet, and will outgrow these fears."

"And learn to climb trees."

"I hope you don't think I climbed that tree out of fear, Bosephus. I merely went up there to get a better view of my audience. One should always rise above his audience. And now let us sing softly together as we go. It will rest us after our day of conquest."

And touching the strings lightly and singing softly together, the friends sought leisurely their evening camp. Here and there a light rustle in the bushes showed that the forest people were listening, and the leaves of the forest whispered in time to their melody.

THE DANCE OF THE FOREST PEOPLE

CHAPTER IV

THE DANCE OF THE FOREST PEOPLE

"Oh! the night was warm and the moon was bright,
And we pitched our camp in the pale moonlight;

In the pale moonlight and the green, green shade,
And we counted up together all the money we had made."

THE little boy jingled the coins in his hands, and hummed and sang to the Bear's soft music. Their camp fire had died down to a few red embers, and the big moon hanging on the tree-tops made all the world white and black, with one bright splash in the brook below. They had finished their supper, and Bosephus, with the needle and thread given to him by old Mis' Todd, had patiently mended by the firelight a small rent in his trouser leg. Horatio, watching him with a grin, had finally remarked :—

"You see, Bo, if you wore clothes like mine you would n't have to do that."

"And if the dog that did that had got his teeth into your clothes you'd have wished they were like mine. Maybe that's why you did n't give him a chance."

"Let's count the money, Bo."

So then they counted up their day's receipts. There was something more than a dollar in all, and Horatio was much pleased.

"I tell you, Bo," he said excitedly, "we've made a fine start. By and by we will earn two or three times that much every day, and be able to start our bear colony before you know it."

"'LET'S COUNT THE MONEY, BO.'"

The little boy fondled the coins over and over. They were the first he had ever earned.

"Ratio," he said at last, "don't you suppose when we get a lot of money—a big lot, I mean—we might give some to those people I used to live with?"

Horatio scowled.

"I thought you said they did n't treat you well and you had to run away."

"Yes, of course, Ratio; but then they were so poor, and may be they 'd have been better to me if I had been able to earn money for them. They did take me out of the poorhouse, you know, and—"

"And you tried to get back again and got lost and fell in with me. Now you are sorry and want to go to them, do you?" and the Bear snorted so fiercely that the little boy trembled.

"Oh, no! Not for the world! I never was so happy in all my life, only I just thought—"

"Then don't think, Bo," interrupted Horatio,

gently. "You are only a little boy. I will do the thinking for this firm. Now for a song, Bo, to soothe us."

So then they played and sang softly together while the moon rose and the fire died out, and the boy poured the money from hand to hand, lovingly.

"Bosephus," said his companion, as they paused, "were those people you lived with nice people? Nice fat people, I mean?"

"Not very. Old Mr. Sugget might have been pretty fat if he'd had more to eat, but Mis' Sugget was n't made to get fat, I know. It was n't her build."

"It was the old man that abused you, was n't it?"

"Well, mostly."

"Knocked you about and half starved you?"

"Sometimes, but then—"

"Wait, please. I have an idea. When we get our bear colony started we'll invite this

Sugget party to visit us. We'll feed him—all he can eat. By and by, when he gets fat—how long do you suppose it will take him to get fat, Bo? Fat enough, I mean?"

"Fat enough for what?" shivered Bo.

Horatio drew the horsehair briskly across the strings and looked up at the moon.

"Fat enough to be entertaining," he grinned, and began singing:—

> "Oh, there was an old man and his ways were mighty mean,
> And he was n't very fat and he was n't very lean,
> Till he went to pay a visit to a colony of bears,
> Then you could n't find a nicer man than he was, anywheres."

While the Bear played the little boy had been watching a slim, moving shadow that seemed to have drifted out from among the heavier shadows into the half-lit open space in front of them. As the music ceased, it drifted back again.

"Play some more, Ratio," he whispered.

Again the Bear played and again the slim shadow appeared in the moonlight and presently another and another. Some of them were slender and graceful; some of them heavier and slower of movement. As the music continued they swung into a half circle and drew closer. Now and then the boy caught a glimpse of two shining sparks that kept time and movement with each. He could hardly breathe in his excitement.

"Look there, Ratio," he whispered.

Horatio did not stir.

"Sh-h!" he said, softly. "My friends—the forest people."

The Bear slackened the music a little as he spoke and the shadows wavered and drew away. Then he livened the strain and they trooped forward again eagerly.

Just then the moon swung clear of the thick trees and the dancers were in its full flood.

The boy watched them with trembling eagerness.

A tall, cat-like creature, erect and graceful, swayed like a phantom in and out among the others, and seemed to lead. As it came directly in front of the musicians it turned full front toward them. It was an immense gray panther.

At any other time Bo would have screamed. Now he was only fascinated. Its step was perfect and its long tail waved behind it, like a silver plume, which the others followed. Two red foxes kept pace with it. Two gray ones, a little to one side, imitated their movements. In the background a family of three bears danced so awkwardly that Bo was inclined to laugh.

"We will teach them to do better than that when we get our colony," he whispered.

Horatio nodded without pausing. The dancers separated, each group to itself, the gray panther in the foreground. Spellbound, the boy watched the beautiful swaying creature. He had been taught to fear the "painter," as it was called in Arkansaw, but he had no fear now. He almost felt that he must himself step out into that enchanted circle and join in the weird dance.

New arrivals stole constantly out of the darkness to mingle in the merrymaking. A little way apart a group of rabbits skipped wildly together, while near them a party of capering wolves had forgotten their taste for blood. Two plump 'coons and a heavy-bodied 'possum, after trying in vain to keep up with the others, were content to sit side by side and look on. Other friends, some of whom the boy did not know, slipped out into the magic circle, and, after watching the others for a moment, leaped madly into the revel. The instinct of the old days had claimed them when the wild beasts of the forest and the wood nymphs trod measures to the

"OTHER FRIENDS SLIPPED INTO THE MAGIC CIRCLE."

pipes of Pan. The boy leaned close to the player.

"The rest of it!" he whispered. "Play the rest of it!"

"I am afraid. They have never heard it before."

"Play it! Play it!" commanded Bo, excitedly.

There was a short, sharp pause at the end of the next bar, then a sudden wild dash into the second half of the tune. The prancing animals stopped as if by magic. For an instant they stood motionless, staring with eyes like coals. Then came a great rush forward, the gray panther at the head. The boy saw them coming, but could not move.

"Sing!" shouted Horatio; "sing!"

For a second the words refused to come. Then they flooded forth in the moonlight. Bo could sing, and he had never sung as he did now.

"Oh, our singing, yes our singing, all our friends
   to us 't is bringing,
For it sets the woods to ringing, and the forest
   people know

That we do not mean to harm them in their
   dancing, nor alarm them—
We are seeking but to charm them with the
   sounds of long ago."

At the first notes of the boy's clear voice the animals hesitated; then they crept up slowly and gathered about to listen. They did not dance to this new strain. Perhaps they wanted to learn it first. Bo sang on and on. The listening audience never moved. Then Horatio played very softly, and the singer lowered his voice until it became like a far off echo. When Bo sang like this he often closed his eyes. He did so now.

The music sank lower and lower, until it died away in a whisper. The boy ceased singing and opening his eyes gazed about him. Here and there he imagined he heard a slight rustle in the leaves, but the gray panther was gone. The frisking rabbits and the capering wolves had vanished. The red and gray foxes, the awkward bears and that rest of that frolicking throng had melted back into the shadows. So far as he could peer into the dim forest he was alone with his faithful friend.

GOOD-BYE TO ARKANSAW

CHAPTER V

GOOD-BYE TO ARKANSAW

"Oh, the wind blows cold and the wind blows raw,
When the night comes on in the Arkansaw—
Yes, the wind blows cold and the snow will fall,
And Bosephus and Horatio must travel through
it all."

THE little boy's voice quavered as he sang, and his teeth chattered. It had been more than two months since he started on his travels with Horatio, and the October nights, even in southern Arkansaw, were beginning to be chilly. The night before he had in some way got separated from his friend's warm furry coat and woke shivering. He kindled a fire now, singing as he worked, while Horatio touched the chords of his violin pensively. He did not feel the cold. Nature was providing him with his winter furs.

"Bo," he said presently, "you 'll have to have some heavier clothes. Either that or we 'll have to go farther South. As for me, you know, I could go to sleep in a hollow tree and not mind the winter, but you could n't do it, and I don't intend to, either, this year; we 're making too much money for that."

Bo laughed in spite of the cold and jingled his pockets. They were more than half full of coin, and he had a good roll of bills in his jacket besides.

"No," he said; "we are getting along too well. We 'll be rich by spring if we keep right on. I 'm thinking, though, that we 'll never be able to get South fast enough if we walk."

"Look here, Bo; you 're not thinking about putting me on that cyclone thing they call a train, are you?"

"Well, not exactly; but yesterday, where we performed, I heard a fellow say that there was a river right close here, and steamboats. You would n't mind a steamboat, would you, Ratio?"

"Of course not. I don't mind anything. I 've always wanted to ride on one of those trains, too, only I knew the people would be frightened at me, and as for a steamboat, why, if I should meet a steamboat coming down the road—"

"But steamboats don't come down the roads, Ratio; they go on the water."

"Water! Water that you drink, and drown things in?"

"Of course! And if the boat goes down we 'll be drowned, too."

Horatio struck a few notes on the violin before replying.

"Bo," he said, presently, "you 're a friend of mine, are n't you? A true friend?"

"Yes, Ratio; you know I am."

"Well, then, don't you go on one of those boats. It would grieve me terribly if anything should happen to you. I might not be able to save you, Bo, and then think how lonely I should be." And Horatio put one paw to his eyes and sobbed.

"Oh, pshaw, Ratio! Why, I can swim like everything. I'm not afraid."

"But you could n't save us both, Bo—I mean, we both could n't save the fiddle—it would get wet. Think—think of the fiddle, Bo!"

The fire was burning brightly by this time and the little boy was getting warm. He laughed and rubbed his hands and began to sing:—

"Oh, we're going down the river on a great big boat,
And Horatio's so excited he can hardly play a note,

THE ARKANSAW BEAR

For he never liked the water and he never learned
    to swim,
And he thinks if he goes sailing now his chances
    will be slim."

Horatio stopped short and snorted angrily.

"I want you to understand," he said, sharply, "that I 'm not afraid of anything. You 'll please remember that night when the forest people danced and you thought your time had come, how I saved you by making you sing. There's nothing I fear. Why, if"—

But what Horatio was about to say will never be known, for at that moment there came such a frightful noise as neither of them had ever heard before. It came from everywhere at once, and seemed to fill all the sky and set the earth to trembling. It was followed by two or three fierce snorts and a dazzling gleam of light through the trees. The little boy was startled, and as for the Bear, he gave one wild look and fled. In his fright he did not notice a small shrub, and, tripping over it, he fell headlong into a clump of briars, where he lay, groaning dismally that he was killed and that the world was coming to an end.

Suddenly Bosephus gave a shout of laughter.

"Get up, Ratio," he called. "It's our steamboat. We're right near the river and did n't know it. They're landing, too, and we can go right aboard."

The groaning ceased and there was a movement among the briars.

Presently Horatio crept out, very much crestfallen, and picked up the violin, which, in his haste, he had dropped.

"Bo," he said, sheepishly, "I never told you about it before, but I am subject to fits. I had one just then. They come on suddenly that way. All my family have them and act strangely at times. I 'm sure you don't think for a moment that I was frightened just now."

"Oh, no; of course not. You merely picked

"HE FELL HEADLONG INTO A CLUMP OF BRIARS."

out that briar patch as a good place to have a fit in. Do you always think the world's coming to an end when you are taken that way?"

"We 'll go right aboard, Bo ; you are a little timid, no doubt, so I 'll lead the way." And Horatio stepped out briskly towards the lights and voices and the landing steamer.

A few steps brought them out to the river bank and a full view of the boat that had crept silently around a bend to the woodyard, where it was halting to take on fuel. The gang-plank had not been pushed out to the bank as yet, but a white ray of light shot from a small window to the dark shore and looked exactly like a narrow board. The boy and the Bear were both deceived by it, and Horatio in his eagerness to show his bravery did not pause to investigate.

"Take the fiddle, Bo," he said, loftily, " and I 'll show you how to get on a boat. You should always be brave, Bosephus."

Bosephus took the instrument, and Horatio,

THE ARKANSAW BEAR

with arms extended as a balance, stepped straight out into nothing and vanished. There was a sudden splash, a growl, a scrambling sound in the shallow water and Horatio's head appeared above the bank. Bosephus, at first frightened, was now doubled with laughter.

"Oh, Ratio," he gasped, "how funny of you to try to walk on a moonbeam!"

Horatio shook himself and sniffed angrily. A wide gang-plank was now being lowered from the boat, and as it touched the bank the boy stepped quickly aboard, followed by the wet, shambling Bear.

> "Oh, there was an Old Bear on a dark, dark night,
> Who tried to walk on a beam of light."

sang Bo, as he crossed the plank,

> "But the beam would n't hold and the Bear broke through,
> And now Horatio follows, as Horatio ought to do."

"Hello!" called a voice. "Where did you come from?"

Bo looked up and saw a brawny man with a group of wondering negroes behind him.

"We are traveling," said Bo, "and we want to go down the river. We can pay our way and will make music for you, too."

"Good boy," said the mate. "Go right up and report to the clerk, then come back down here, and after we get this wood loaded we'll give you some supper and you can give us a show."

On the upper deck the few passengers gathered around and made much of the arrivals. All asked questions at once, and Bo answered as best he could. Horatio kept silent—he never talked except when he was alone with Bo. The boy kept his hand on the Bear's head, and when the boat backed away and puffed down stream he felt his big friend tremble, but a little later, when they had had a good supper, Ratio's fear passed off, and on the lower deck, where all hands collected, the friends gave an entertainment that not only won for them free passage down the river, but a good collection besides.

"THE NEGROES PATTED AND DANCED CRAZILY."

It was far in the night when the performance ended. The officers, passengers, and crew kept calling for more, and the travelers were anxious

THE ARKANSAW BEAR

to please them. The negroes went wild over the music, and patted and danced crazily whenever Horatio played. Finally Bo sang a good-night song:—

"Now, we 've had a lot of music, and we 've had some supper, too,
And we 're sailing down the river in a little steam canoe,

And we love to be obliging with our music, but it seems
That we ought to go a-sailing to the land of pleasant dreams.

"And I must not fail to mention we enjoy your kind attention,
And the favors you have shown to us have filled us with delight,

And to-morrow we will play for you and sing
our songs so gay for you,
But now you will excuse us if we say—good
—night."

Bosephus and Horatio were both offered staterooms on the upper deck, but Horatio preferred to sleep outside, and the little boy said he would sleep there also. Horatio sat up for some moments after Bo had stretched himself to rest, looking at the dark wooded banks and the starlight on the water behind them.

"Bo," he said, at last, "we are going to see the world now, sure enough."

"Yes, Ratio," was the sleepy answer.

"Bo, do you suppose our camp-fire is still burning back yonder?"

No answer.

"I hate to leave old Arkansaw, don't you, Bo?"

But the little boy was in the land of dreams.

AN EXCITING RACE

CHAPTER VI

AN EXCITING RACE

" Sailing down the river so early in the morn,
Sailing down the river so early in the morn,
Sailing down the river so early in the morn,
Never was so happy since the day that I was born."

THE boat on which Horatio and Bosephus had taken their passage made no landings during the night, and the little boy and the big Bear slept soundly on the deck together. Rather too soundly, as will be seen later. At daybreak the next morning Bosephus was wide awake, singing softly and watching through the mist the queer forms of the cypress trees, with the long Spanish moss swinging from the limbs. Horatio, hearing the singing, rubbed his eyes and sat up. He had never been so far South before, so the scenery was new to both of them, and when they came to open spaces and saw that the shores were only a few inches higher than the river, and that fields of waving green came right to the water's edge, they were both pleased and surprised at this new world. The climate had changed, too, and the air was warm and springlike.

"I tell you, Bo," said Horatio, grandly, "there's nothing like travel. You're a lucky boy, Bo, to fall in with me. Why, the way you've come out in the last few months is wonderful. Of course, there is a good deal of room yet for improvement, and there are still some things that you are rather timid of, but when I remember how you looked the first minute I saw you, and then to see the sociable way you sit up and talk to me now, you really don't seem like the same boy, Bosephus, you really don't."

"THE LITTLE BOY AND THE BIG BEAR SLEPT SOUNDLY."

The little boy leaned up close to his companion.

"Oh, there was a little boy and his name was Bo,"

he sang softly, remembering their first meeting.

"Went out into the woods when the moon was low,"

added the Bear, strumming lightly the strings of the violin.

"And he met an Old Bear that was hungry for a snack,
   And the folks are still awaiting for Bosephus to come back,"

they continued together in a half whisper.

"Ratio," said the little boy, confidentially, "did you really intend to—to have me—you know, Ratio—for—for supper until I taught you the tune? Did you, Ratio?"

Horatio gazed away across a broad cane field, where the first streak of sunrise was beginning to show.

THE ARKANSAW BEAR

"For the boy became the teacher of the kind and
  gentle creature
  Who could play upon the fiddle in a very
  skilful way,"

he sang dreamily, and then both together once more :—

"Now he 'll never, never leave him, and he 'll
  never, never grieve him,
  And we 're singing here together at the break
  —of—day."

"This is very pleasant traveling," commented Horatio, thoughtfully. "It beats walking, at least for speed and comfort. Of course, there are a number of places we cannot reach by boat," he added, regretfully.

"Not in Southern Louisiana, Ratio. I've heard that there 's a regular tangle of rivers and bayous all over the country, and that boats go everywhere."

Horatio looked pleased.

"Are n't you glad now, Bo," he said, proudly,

"that I proposed this boat business? I have always wanted to travel this way. I was afraid at first that you might not take to it very well, and when that whistle blew last night I could see that you were frightened. It was too bad that I should have had a fit just then, or I might have calmed you. You saw how anxious I was to go aboard. Of course, in being over-brave I made a slight mistake. I am always that way. All my family are. One really ought to be less reckless about some things, but somehow none of my family ever knew what fear was. We—"

But just then the boat concluded to land, and the morning stillness was torn into shreds by its frightful whistle. Horatio threw up his paws and fell backward on the deck, where he lay clawing the air wildly. Then he stuffed his paws into his ears and howled as he kicked with his hind feet. Bo stood over him and shouted that there was no danger, but his voice made no sound in that awful thunder. All at once Horatio sprang up and jammed his head under Bo's arm, trembling like a jellyfish. Then the noise stopped, and with one or two more hoarse shouts ceased entirely.

"It's all right, Ratio, come out!" said Bo, trying to stop laughing.

Horatio felt of his ears a moment to see that they were still there, while he looked skittishly in the direction of the dreadful whistle and started violently at the quick snorts of the escaping steam.

"Bo," he said, faintly, "do all boats do that?"

"Oh, yes! Some worse than others. This one isn't very bad."

"I'm sorry, Bo, for it is a great drawback to travel where one is subject to fits as I am. It seems to bring them on. And it is not kind of you to laugh at my affliction, either, Bosephus," he added, for Bo had dropped down on the deck, where he was rolling and holding his sides.

All at once the boy lay perfectly still. Then

"HORATIO LAY PAWING THE AIR WILDLY."

he sprang up with every bit of laugh gone out of his face. His left hand grasped the outside of his jacket, while with his right hand he dived down into the inside pocket like mad. The Bear watched him anxiously.

"What is it, Bo? Have you got one, too?" he asked.

"Horatio!" gasped the boy. "Our money! It's gone!"

"Gone! Gone! Where?"

"Stolen. Some of those niggers did it while we were asleep!"

The bear reflected a moment. Then he said thoughtfully:

"Do you suppose, Bo, it was that nice fat one?"

"I shouldn't wonder a bit. I saw him watch every penny I took in last night."

Horatio licked out his tongue eagerly.

"Could I have him if it was?" he asked, hungrily.

"Have him! How?" said Bo. Then he shuddered. "Oh! no, not that way—of course not. But I'll tell you, Ratio," he added, "we'll make him believe that you can, and frighten him into giving up the money."

Horatio frowned.

"I don't like make-believes," he grumbled. "Can't we let the money go this time and not have any make-believe?"

"Not much—we want that money right now, before the boat lands; then we'll go ashore and get out of such a crowd. Come, Ratio."

No one was stirring on the upper deck as yet, but the crew was collected below, where the second mate was shouting orders as the boat swung slowly into the bank. The boy and Bear dashed down the stairs.

"Wait!" shouted Bo to the officer. "Somebody on this boat last night stole our money, and I want my Bear to find him. It won't take but a minute, for he can tell a thief at

"'HORATIO! OUR MONEY! IT IS GONE!'"

sight when he's mad and hungry, and he's mad now, and hungry for dark meat" The boy looked straight into the crowd of negroes, while the Bear growled fiercely and fixed his eye on the fat darky.

The crew fell back and the fat darky with a howl started to run.

"That's the one! That's the thief!" shouted Bo, and with a snarl Horatio bounded away in pursuit. Down the narrow gangway to the stern of the boat, then in a circle around a lot of cotton, they ran like mad, the Bear getting closer to the negro every minute. Then back again to the bow in a straight stretch, the thief blue with fright and Horatio's eyes shining. The rest of the crew looked on and cheered. Suddenly, as the fat darky passed Bo, he jerked a sack from his pocket and flung it behind him.

"Dar's yo' money! Dar's yo' money!" he shouted. "Call off yo' B'ar!"

But that was not so easy. Bosephus shouted

frantically at Horatio, but he did not seem to hear. His blood was up, and his taste for dark meat was stronger than his love of money. As the two came clattering around the second time he was so close to his prey that with a quick swipe he got quite a piece of his shirt. With a wild yell the fat fugitive leaped over into the river and struck out for shore.

Horatio paused. His half open jaws were dripping and his eyes red and fiery with disappointment. Bo went up to him gently.

"Come, Ratio," he whispered.

The Bear paid no heed. He was watching his escaped prey, who had reached the shore and was disappearing in a great canefield.

"Come!" Bo whispered again. "We'll go ashore, too."

Horatio wheeled eagerly. The gang-plank was being lowered, and he hurried Bo out on it, so that when it touched the bank he was all ready to give chase again.

"No, wait; some music first," said Bo. "I have thought of some new lines for the second part of the tune."

For a moment Horatio hesitated. Then the temptation of the music was stronger even than

"THE FAT FUGITIVE LEAPED INTO THE RIVER."

his appetite, and, throwing his violin into position, he began to play. The passengers, roused by the excitement, had gathered on the upper deck. The crew coming ashore below paused to listen.

"Oh! there was a fat darky with an appetite for wealth,
And the only way to get it was to capture it by stealth,

But when it came to keep it, his chances were so small,
He concluded that he really did n't care for it at all.

For we placed him and we faced him, and my bear Horatio chased him—
In a manner most surprising he pursued him to and fro—

And we hope we do not grieve you, but we feel that we must leave you,
For the Southern sun is rising, and we 're bound—to—go."

The crew cheered and the passengers on the upper deck shouted and waved their handkerchiefs.

"Don't go!" they called. "Don't leave us!" But the friends turned their faces to the East and set out on a broad white road that led away to the sunrise.

HORATIO'S MOONLIGHT ADVENTURE

CHAPTER VII

HORATIO'S MOONLIGHT ADVENTURE

" Rooster in de chicken coop crowin' foh day,
Horses in de stable goin' 'Nay, nay, nay!'

Ducks in de yard goin' 'Quack, quack, quack!'
Guineas in de tree tops goin' Rack-pot-rack!'"

DURING the two weeks since they had come to the land of sugar-cane Horatio and Bosephus had learned some of the old negro songs of Louisiana, and sang them to their own music. They were doing so now as they marched along the bank of a quiet bayou, where the blue grass came to the water's edge and the long Spanish moss from big live oak trees swung down twenty feet or more till it almost touched the water. They had had a good day and were going to camp.

"Bo," said the Bear presently, "we are doing well. We are making money, Bo."

"Fifty dollars since we left the boat," said the little boy.

"These fat babies—little darky babies—are very—amusing, too, Bosephus; don't you think so?" Horatio added, nodding in the direction of some they were just then passing.

"I notice that you think so," said Bo, dryly. "If you 'll take my advice, though, you won't show any special fondness for them. People might not understand your ways, you know, and besides," he added, with a grin, "I 've heard say these darkies down here are mighty fond of bear meat, and there 's such a lot of them—"

"'THESE LITTLE DARKY BABIES ARE VERY—AMUSING.'"

"Don't mention it, Bo; I never dreamed of such a thing as you are hinting at."

Horatio drew his bow hastily across the strings and began singing—

"Keemo, kimo, kilgo, kayro,
  Horses in de stable goin' 'Nay, nay, nay!'

Rop strop, periwinkle, little yaller nigger,
  Cum a rop strop bottle till the break of day."

The sun was just setting behind a large, white, old-fashioned sugar house, where the bayou turned, and made it look like an ancient castle. The little boy sighed. He had never believed that any country could be so beautiful as this, and he wanted to stay in it forever. Horatio liked it, too. They had played and danced at many of the sugar houses, and the

THE ARKANSAW BEAR

Bear had been given, everywhere, all the waste sugar he could eat. He was fond of the green cane, also, and was nearly always chewing a piece when they were not busy with a performance. But the big fellow had never quite overcome his old savage nature, and the race on the steamboat had roused it more fiercely than ever. The fat pickaninnies were a constant temptation to him, and it had taken all Bo's watchfulness to keep him out of dreadful mischief. Bo never feared for himself. Horatio loved him and had even become afraid of him. It was for Horatio that he feared, for he knew that death would be sure and swift if one of the pickaninnies was even so much as scratched, not to mention anything worse that might happen. Again the little boy sighed as they turned into a clean, grassy place and made ready for camp.

Long after Bosephus was asleep Horatio sat by the dying camp fire, thinking. By and by

"EVERY LITTLE WAY HE PAUSED."

he rose and walked out to the bank of the bayou and looked toward the sugar house that lay white in the moonlight, half a mile away. Then he went back to where Bo was asleep and picked up the violin. Then he laid it down again, as though he had changed his mind, and slipped away through the shadows in the direction of the old sugar house. He said to himself that, as they were going in that direction and would stop there next day, he might as well see how the road went and what kind of a place it was. He did not own, even to himself, that it was the negro cabins and fat pickaninnies that were in his mind, and that down in his heart was a wicked and savage purpose. Every little way he paused and seemed about to turn back, but he kept on. By and by he drew near the sugar house and saw the double row of white-washed huts in the moonlight. It was later than he had supposed and the crowds of little darkies that were usually playing outside had gone to bed. He sighed and was about to turn back when suddenly he saw something capering about near the shed of the sugar house. He slipped up nearer and a fierce light came into his eyes. It was a little negro boy doing a hoo-doo dance in the moonlight.

Suddenly the little fellow turned and saw the Bear glaring at him. Horatio was between him and the cabins. The boy gave one wild shriek and dashed through a small open door that led into the blackness of the sugar house, the Bear following close behind. It was one of the old Creole sugar houses where the syrup is poured out into shallow open vessels to cool and harden. The little darkey knew his way and Horatio did n't. He stumbled and fell, and growled and tried to follow the flying shadow that was skipping and leaping and begging, "Oh, Mars Debbil! Oh, please, Mars Debbil, lemme go dis time, an' I nevah do so no mo'. Nevah do no mo' hoo-doo,

"HORATIO WAS BETWEEN HIM AND THE CABINS."

Mars Debbil; oh, please, Mars Debbil, lemme go!"

But Horatio was getting closer and closer, and in another moment would seize him. Then, suddenly, something happened. The Bear stumbled and, half falling, stepped into one of the big shallow wooden vessels. He felt his hind feet break through something like crusted ice and sink a foot or more into a heavy, thick substance below. When he tried to lift them they only sank deeper. Then he knew what was the matter. He had stepped into a mass of hardening sugar and was a prisoner! His forefeet were free, but he dared not struggle with them for fear of getting them fast, too. The little darkey, who thought the devil had stopped to rest, was huddled together in a corner, not daring to move. Horatio remembered Bo sleeping safely in their camp and began to weep for his own wickedness. In the morning men would come with axes and guns. Why had he not heeded Bo? Half seated on the crusted sugar he gave himself up to sorrow and despair.

* * * * *

It was early morning when Bo awoke. He was surprised to see that Horatio was not beside him, for the boy was usually first awake. He called loudly. Then, as the moments passed and the Bear did not come, he grew uneasy. Suddenly a terrible suspicion flashed over him. He sprang to his feet and seizing the violin that lay beside him, set forth on a run in the direction of the white sugar house. He knew Horatio would go there because it was nearest, and he felt certain that something dreadful had happened. The incident of the day before made him almost sure of Horatio's errand, and he feared the worst. No doubt they had caught and killed him by this time, and what would he do now without his faithful friend?

He ran faster and faster. As he drew near

the sugar house he heard a great commotion. For a moment he stopped. If Horatio had done something terrible and they had caught him perhaps it would be dangerous to interfere. The next moment he rushed on. Horatio was his friend and he would save his life if possible, unless—— He did not think any further, but flew on. As he dashed into the cane yard he saw crowds gathering and men running with axes and clubs. Others had guns and cane knives, and all were crowding toward the big doors of the sugar house, that were now thrown open. Inside he heard shouts, mingled with Horatio's fierce growls. His friend was still alive.

Without pausing, he rushed through the doors and saw a circle of negro men gathered about the big wooden trough where the Bear, a prisoner, was snapping and growling and trying to get free. The little pickaninny who, in spite of his fright, had slept all night in the

THE ARKANSAW BEAR

corner, was there, too, and the men with axes and other weapons had entered with Bo. There was not a second to be lost.

"Wait!" screamed Bo, "wait!" And, tearing through the astonished crowd, he thrust the violin into Horatio's hands.

"Play!" he shouted. "Play for your worthless life!"

Horatio did not need to be told again. He reached for the violin and bow, and, sitting in the now solid sugar, struck the strings wildly.

"Rooster in de chicken coop, crowin' foh day,
  Horses in de stable goin' 'Nay, nay, nay,'
  Ducks in de yard goin' 'Quack, quack, quack!'
  Guineas in de tree tops goin' 'Rack-pot-rack!'"

Horatio fiddled furiously, while Bo shouted and sang and the crowd joined in. They all knew this song, and as they sang they forgot all else. Axes and clubs and guns were dropped as young and old fell into the swing of the music.

"Keemo, kimo, kilgo, kayro;
Fleero, fliro, flav-o-ray;
Rop strop, periwinkle, little yaller nigger,
Cum a rop strop bottle till de break—of—day!"

You could hear the noise for a mile. They danced and shouted and sang, and work was forgotten. After a long time, when they were tired out, Bo took one of the axes and carefully broke the now solid sugar away from Ratio's feet and set him free. Then they brought water and washed his hind paws, and he danced for them.

After dinner, when the friends started out on their journey, the crowd followed them for nearly a mile. When all were gone Horatio turned to Bo and said:—

"I am glad you came just as you did, Bo."

"I should rather think you would be," said Bo, grimly.

"Because," continued Horatio, "if you had n't I might have damaged some of those fellows, and I know you would n't have liked that, Bosephus."

He looked at the little boy very humbly as he said this, expecting a severe lecture. But the little boy made no reply, and down in his heart the big Bear at that moment made a solemn and good resolve.

SWEET AND SOUR

CHAPTER VIII

SWEET AND SOUR

"Oh, we're down in the land where the jasmine blows,
And the cypress waves and the orange grows,

And the song bird nests in the climbing rose—
And all the girls are beautiful, and milk and honey flows."

HORATIO paused in his playing and looked at Bosephus, who was ready to sing another stanza.

"Look here, Bo," he said gravely, "that sounds very pretty and may be very good poetry and true enough, but I would n't get to singing too much about jasmine and song birds and climbing roses if I were you, and especially girls. You are only a little boy, and besides, I can't see that there is any difference in girls, except that some are plump and some are not, and that is n't any difference to me, now," and the Bear sighed and strummed on his violin gently.

"Oh, pshaw, Ratio! There's lots of difference. Some girls are yellow and sour as a lemon, while some are as pink and sweet and blooming as a creole rose"—

"Bosephus," interrupted the Bear gravely, "you've got a touch of the swamp fever. Let me see your tongue!"

Bo stuck out his tongue.

"My tongue's all right," he grinned. "That kind of fever's in the heart."

Horatio looked alarmed.

"You must take something for it right away,

Bo," he declared. "I can't have you singing silly songs about jasmine and cypress and girls in milk and honey. You know we have n't seen any honey since we left Arkansaw, and I'd travel all the way back there on foot to rob one good honey tree. I'm getting tired of so much of this stuff they call sugar and cane and the like!"

"Why, they have honey here, Ratio, too. I have n't seen any bee trees, but I've seen plenty of bees. I suppose they are in hives—boxes that people keep for them to live in."

"Where do they have those boxes, Bo?"

"Well, in their yards mostly; generally out by the back fence."

"Could we rob them?"

"Well, I should n't like to try it."

The Bear walked along some distance in silence. The boy was also thinking and singing softly to himself. He was very happy. Presently he looked up and saw just ahead, in a field near the road, a tree loaded with oranges.

"Look, Ratio!" he said. "Don't you wish we had some of those?"

The Bear looked up and began to lick out his tongue.

"Climb over and get some, Bo," he said eagerly.

"Not much. I have n't forgotten the roasting ears and the watermelon we got from old man Todd in Arkansaw. We might go to the house and ask for some."

"Nonsense, Bosephus. Watch me!"

He handed Bo the fiddle, and running lightly to the hedge cleared it at a bound.

"Fine!" shouted Bo.

Horatio, without pausing, hurried over to the tree.

"Funny they should leave those oranges so late," thought the little boy as he watched him.

Swinging himself to the first limb, the Bear

shook off a lot of the fine yellow fruit, and climbing down, gathered in his arms all he could carry. As he did so there came a loud barking of dogs, and without looking behind him he started to run. He dropped a few of the oranges, but kept straight on, the two huge dogs that had appeared getting closer and closer. As he reached the hedge he once more made a grand leap, but the oranges prevented him doing so well as before. His foot caught in the top branches and he rolled over and over in the dusty road, the oranges flying in every direction. The dogs behind the hedge barked and raged.

Horatio rose, dusty and panting, but triumphant.

"You see, Bo," he said, "what it is to be brave. You can fill your pockets now with these delicious oranges."

He picked up one as he spoke, and brushing off the dust, bit it in half cheerfully. Then Bo, who was watching him, saw a strange thing take place. The half orange flew out of the Bear's mouth as from a popgun, and his face became so distorted that the boy thought his friend was having a spasm. Suddenly he whirled, and making a rush at the fallen oranges, began to kick them in every direction, coughing and spitting every second. The two dogs looking over the hedge stopped barking to enjoy the fun. One of the oranges rolled to Bo's feet. He picked it up and smelled it. Then rubbing it on his coat, he bit into it. It was not a large bite, but it was enough. The tears rolled from his eyes and every tooth in his head jumped. Such a mixture of stinging, sour, and bitter he had never dreamed of. It grabbed him by the throat and shook him until his bones cracked. The top of his head seemed coming loose, and his ears fairly snapped. Then he realized what Horatio must be suffering, and **laughed in spite of himself.**

"HE BIT IT IN HALF CHEERFULLY."

"They are mock oranges, Ratio," he shouted, "and they are mocking us for stealing them!"

Horatio had seated himself by the roadside, and was snorting and clawing at his tongue.

"I must have some honey, Bo," he said, "to take away that dreadful taste. You must find me some honey, Bo."

"You see, Ratio," said the little boy, "it does n't pay to take things."

"Bosephus," said the Bear, "a man who will plant a tree like that so near the road deceives willfully and should be punished."

They walked along slowly, the two dogs barking after them from behind the hedge.

Just beyond the next bend in the road a beautiful plantation came into view. They turned into the cane yard, and immediately the work hands surrounded them. Horatio felt better by this time, and they began a performance. First Bo sang, and then Horatio gave a gymnastic exhibition. Then, at last, Bo sang a closing verse as follows:—

"Now our little show is ended, and we hope you
  think it splendid,
And we trust we've not offended or displeased
  you anywhere;

You have paid us to be funny, and we thank
  you for the money,
But I'd like a little honey for the Old—
  Black—Bear."

Horatio smiled when he heard this, and the planter, who was listening, sent one of the servants to the house. He came out soon with a piece of fresh honey on a plate. He offered it to Horatio, who handed Bo the violin, and, seizing the plate, swallowed the honey at one gulp. This made the crowd shout and laugh, and then

Bo shook hands with the planter and said good-bye, and all the darkies came up and wanted to shake hands, too. When he had shaken hands all around the little boy turned to look for Horatio. He was nowhere in sight. The others had not noticed him slip away.

Bo was troubled. When Horatio disappeared like that it meant mischief. He had promised reform as to pickaninnies, but Bo was never quite sure. He was about to ask the people to run in every direction in search of his comrade when there was a sudden commotion in the back door yard, and a moment later a black figure dashed through the gate with something under its arm. It was Horatio! The crowd of darkies took one look and scattered. The thing under Horatio's arm was a square box-looking affair, and out of it was streaming a black, living cloud.

"Bees!" shouted the people as they fled. "Bees! Bees!"

Bo understood instantly. The taste of honey had made Horatio greedy for more. He had gone in search of it and returned with hive and all. There was a clump of tall weeds just behind the little boy, and he dropped down into them. They hid him from view, and none too soon, for the Bear dashed past, snorting and striking at the swarm of stingers that not only covered him, but fiercely attacked everything in sight. Howls began to come from some of the hands that had failed to find shelter in time, and Bo, peeping out between the weeds, saw half a dozen darkies frantically trying to open the big door of the sugar-house, which had been hastily closed by those within, while the angry bees were pelting furiously at the unfortunates.

As for Horatio, he was coated with bees that were trying to sting through his thick fur. He did not mind them at first, but presently they began to get near his eyes. With a snarl he

"THE BEAR DASHED PAST, STRIKING AT THE SWARM."

dropped the hive and began to paw and strike with both hands. Then they swarmed about him worse than ever, and, half-blinded, he began to run around and around, with no regard as to direction. Every darky in sight fled like the wind. Some of them ran out of the gate and down the road, and without seeing them, perhaps, the Bear suddenly leaped the fence and set out in the same direction. Glancing back, they saw him coming, and began to shriek and scatter into the fields.

Bo waited some minutes; then noticing that the maddened insects were no longer buzzing viciously over him, he crept out and followed. He still held the violin and was glad enough to get away from the plantation. The bees had followed the fugitive, and the boy kept far enough behind to be out of danger. By and by he met bees coming back, but perhaps they were tired or thought he belonged to another crowd, for they did not molest him. A mile further on he found Horatio sitting on the road rocking and groaning and throwing dust on himself. His eyes and nose were swollen in great knots, and his ears were each puffed up like little balloons. The bees had left him, but his sorrow was at its height.

"Hello, Ratio! Having fun all alone?" asked Bo, as he came up.

"Oh, Bo, this has been an awful day!" was the wailing reply. "First those terrible oranges and then these millions and millions of murderous bees. And now I am blind, Bo, and dying. Tell me, Bo, how do I look?"

"Oh, you look all right. Your nose looks like a big potato and your ears like two little ones. I can't tell you how your eyes are, for they don't show, but your whole skin looks as if it had been stuffed full of apples and put on in a hurry."

"Bo," said Horatio, meekly, "did you bring the fiddle?"

"HIS EYES AND NOSE WERE SWOLLEN IN GREAT KNOTS."

"Well, yes; I thought it might happen that we'd need it again."

Horatio put out his paw for it. The boy gave it to him and he ran the bow gently over the strings.

"Sing, Bo," he pleaded. "Sing that song about jasmine and cypress and climbing roses. It will soothe me. Sing about girls, too, if you want to, but leave out the oranges, Bo, and put in something else besides honey in the last line."

"Ratio," said Bo, "you've got a touch of the swamp fever. Let me see your tongue!"

IN JAIL AT LAST

CHAPTER IX

IN JAIL AT LAST

"Oh, the sky is blue and the sun is high,
And the days roll 'round, and the weeks go
by—"

BO," interrupted Horatio, softly, "what's that over there on the bank that looks like a man all in a wad?"

The little boy was singing along through the sweet Louisiana afternoon, putting into his song whatever came into his head:—

"And I turn, and I look, and what do I see?
Someone's left his bundle by a live oak tree."

"What do you suppose is in that bundle, Bo?" asked the Bear, anxiously.

"Oh, I don't know. Old clothes, from the looks of it. The owner is n't far off.

"When a coat and vest and hat, and pair of
    trousers you espy,
  You can bet your bottom dollar there 's a man
    close by."

Horatio looked in every direction. Then he walked over to the clothes.

"Why," said Bo, following; "I guess somebody's taking a swim. Come on, Ratio. Remember the honey and the oranges."

But the Bear was curious. He picked up the hat and set it on his head. Bo laughed lazily. Then Horatio laid down his violin and slipped one arm into the waistcoat, trying vainly to reach with the other. Bo good-naturedly helped him. The little boy felt in the humor for fun, and Horatio looked too comical.

"Better not put on the coat," said Bo. "It might not be big enough, and if you tore it the owner would make us pay for it."

"'IS MY HAT BECOMING, BO?'"

But Horatio was excited.

"Hurry, Bo! Help me on with it. How do I look, Bo? I think I'll dress this way all the time, hereafter. Is my hat becoming, Bo?"

"Oh, there was an Old Bear in a hat and a coat,"

sang Bo, but he got no further, for suddenly close by there was a loud yell, and without pausing to look behind Horatio made a wild dash in the other direction, followed by the little boy. Glancing back as they ran, Bo saw that they were pursued by a tall white man. He had paused only a second to slip on his boots and trousers, and was coming after them full speed. In one hand he carried a revolver, in the other Horatio's violin.

"Shed 'em!" he shouted. "Shed them clothes or I'll shoot!"

"Shed 'em!" echoed Bo. "Shed 'em, Horatio!"

The bear slipped off the coat and flung it behind him.

"Shed 'em!" shouted the man again, and the waistcoat followed.

"I won't give up the hat, Bo!" panted Horatio.

But Horatio was mistaken, for that instant the world beneath his feet suddenly opened and he disappeared. Before the boy could check himself he plunged after the Bear, and was struggling in the deep waters of a bayou that came to a level with the bank and was covered thickly and hidden by fallen leaves. Rising to the surface he found Horatio clinging to a fallen tree, and the man, who had now overtaken them, holding out a limb, which the little boy gladly seized. The hat had been already rescued.

"Well, you're a nice pair!" said their captor. "To run away with a man's clothes and then go headlong into the bayou and get his hat all

"'SHED THEM CLOTHES OR I'LL SHOOT!'"

wet! I 'm glad you did n't have that fiddle, or you 'd a-ruined it. I 've bin wantin' a good fiddle a long time, an' this here looks like a good one. Come out o' that, now, an' we'll take a walk up toward the jail. I happen to be constable of this here community."

Bo groaned as he was dragged to shore. He did not mind the wetting, for the weather was warm, but now they had lost the violin and would be taken to jail. Of course they would lose all their money. Perhaps Horatio would be killed. The Bear only blinked and shook himself when he had been also towed to the bank and had scrambled out.

"I hope you won't take us to jail, sir," said Bo. "My Bear was mischievous, but he did n't mean any harm, and I have a little money I 'll give you if you 'll return us the violin and let us go."

"You come along with me!" answered the man, sternly. "It 'll take more money than you 've got to pay your fine, an' as fer that chap, we don't want no bears roamin' loose aroun' here. March on ahead there, an' don't try none o' your tricks."

The constable cocked his revolver, and boy and Bear hurriedly started in the direction of the village that showed above the trees about a mile further on.

Bo was afraid to speak to their captor again, and as he never talked with Horatio except when they were alone, they marched along disconsolately and in silence. Now and then the man strummed on the violin and chuckled to himself.

When they got to the village everybody came out to look at them. The man called out his story as they went along, and the people laughed and jeered. Heretofore the friends had entered Louisiana villages in triumph. Now, for the first time, they came dishonored and disgraced. Poor Horatio looked very downcast. He knew that he was to blame for it all.

When they got to the court room they found that the Justice of the Peace was away fishing, so they were lodged in jail for the night. It was only a little one-room affair, with two small iron-barred windows, quite high from the ground. Boys climbed up and looked through these windows and threw stones and coal at Horatio, who huddled in a corner. By and by the officer came with a plate of supper for Bo. He drove the boys away and left the friends together. There was no supper for the Bear, so the little boy divided with him.

"Bo," said Horatio, tearfully, "it was my fault. They'll let you go, and, and—I hope they'll give you my skin, Bo."

Then they went to sleep.

*   *   *   *   *

Early the next morning there was a crowd

around the jail. The Justice had returned and the people wanted to see the fun. The friends were hustled into court by the constable, the crowd stepping back to let Horatio pass. The Justice was rather a young man and had a good-natured face, which made Bo more hopeful. But when they heard the constable make his charge against them, both lost heart. They were accused of stealing and damages and a lot of other things that they could not understand. The Justice listened and then turned to the prisoners.

"What have you to say for yourselves?" he asked, looking straight at Bo. At first the little boy tried to speak and could not. The court room was still—everyone waiting to hear what he was about to say. All at once an idea came to him.

"Please, sir," he trembled, "if you will let my Bear have the violin we will plead our case together."

"What violin? What does the boy mean?" asked the Justice, turning to the constable.

"Oh, an ole fiddle they dropped when they took my clothes. I lef' it down 't the house this morning."

Bo's heart sank. It was their only chance. He was about to give up when suddenly there came another gleam of hope, though very faint. Wheeling quickly toward the sorrow-stricken Bear he shouted:—

"Perform for them, Horatio! Perform!"

The words acted on Horatio like a shock of electricity. He straightened up with a snort that caused the crowd to fall back, knocking each other over like dominoes. Then he made a bound into the open space and stood on his head. Then with a spring backward he landed on his feet, and waved a bow to the Justice! Another bound and he was walking on his hands and then, after another bow to the Court, he turned a series of somersaults so rapidly that he looked like a great wheel! When he landed on his feet this time, and bowed once more to the Court, the crowd broke out into a mighty cheer of applause.

"Order!" shouted the Justice. "Order!"

It grew still, and the little boy looked at the Court anxiously.

"Please, your Honor," he said, humbly, "that's our case."

"Case!" roared the Justice. "Well, I should say that was a case of fits and revolution."

At this the crowd cheered again until they were rapped to order by the Court.

"I sentence you," he said solemnly, and looking sternly at Horatio, "to sudden and disagreeable death!"

He paused, and Horatio staggered against Bo, who was very pale.

"To sudden death," continued the Court, "if I catch you running off and falling in the water with any more of my officers' clothes. And I now fine you for the first offense, a performance on the common for the whole town! Court is adjourned! Show begins at once! Constable, bring that fiddle!"

With a wild shout the people poured outside. Many scrambled over each other to get near Bosephus and the wonderful Bear, and when the violin was brought and the show had begun every soul in the village was gathered on the common.

That night, when all was over, the little boy and the Bear were the guests of the Justice, who owned a fine plantation adjoining the village. During the evening he had a long talk with Bo, and seemed greatly impressed with the little boy's natural ability and shrewdness. When they parted the next morning he said:—

"Remember, if you ever feel like giving up travel, come back here and I'll send you to school and college and make a man of you."

"I 'll remember," said Bo, as they shook

hands. A crowd had gathered to see the travelers off. The constable was among them, and as they disappeared around a bend in the road he waved and shouted with the rest.

"Bosephus," said Horatio, gravely, "I hope you don't think of deserting me. Remember how many close places I have helped you out of. This last one was a little the closest of all, Bosephus, and I shudder to think where you might have been to-day if it had not been for me."

"That's so," said the little boy, solemnly. "I don't suppose they'd have even given me your skin, Ratio."

AN AFTERNOON'S FISHING

13.—Arkansaw Bear

CHAPTER X

AN AFTERNOON'S FISHING

"Sitting on a bank where the bullfrogs dream—
Sitting on the shore of a deep, deep stream—
Sitting on a log and waiting for a bite—
Bound to catch our supper, if we fish—all—
night."

THE little boy was holding a long cane pole that he had cut as they came along, on the small end of which he had fastened a hook and line, baited with a lively worm. The Bear was leaning back against a tree and watching him lazily.

"Bo," said he, presently, "I should n't wonder if that singing of yours scared the fish all away."

"I would n't say that to you, Ratio. I know if you 'd wake up and take the fiddle and play some they 'd walk right out on the bank."

The Bear laughed, sleepily. He was in a comfortable position and the warm afternoon sun was soothing. He hummed some negro lines he had heard :—

"When yo' wan' to ketch fish yo' mus' jes' set an' wait—
When yo' wan' to ketch fish yo' mus' spit on yo' bait—
When yo' wan' to ketch fish yo' mus' git across de tide,
Foy dey 's alw'ys bettah fishin' on de oth—ah—side."

"I should n't wonder if you were right, Ratio," assented Bo, anxiously. "It does look better over there, only there 's no way to get across except this slippery-looking, rotten old log, and I don't feel much like trying that."

"Walk out on it a little way, Bo," said

Horatio, getting interested, "and throw your line over there by that cypress snag. That looks like a good place."

Bosephus rose cautiously, and, balancing himself with the long cane pole, edged his way a few inches at a time toward the middle of the stream, pausing every little way to be sure that the log showed no sign of yielding. He could swim, but he did not wish for a wetting, and besides there were a good many alligators in these Louisiana waters and some very fierce snapping turtles. He had heard the negroes say that alligators were particularly fond of boys, and that snapping turtles never let go till it thundered. He had no wish to furnish supper for an alligator and there were no signs of a thunder storm. Hence he advanced with great prudence. When he had nearly reached the centre Horatio called to him.

"Try it from there, Bo! Your line's long enough to reach!"

The little boy steadied himself by a limb that projected from the log and swung his line in the direction the Bear had indicated. Then he waited, holding his breath almost, and watching his float, which lay silently on the water. Horatio was watching, too, with half-closed eyes, and now and then giving instructions.

"Pull it a little more to the right, Bo—nearer that root," he whispered.

Bosephus obeyed, but the float still lay silently on the water.

"Draw it a little toward you, Bo; sometimes when they think it's going away they make a rush for it."

Again the little boy did as directed, but without result.

"Lift out your bait and see if it's all right. Now fling it a little further toward the bank."

Bo lifted out the bait, which was still lively and untouched, and flung it far over toward the other shore. Then he waited in silence once more, but there was no sign of even so much as a nibble.

"Oh, pshaw, Ratio!" he said at last, impatiently. "I don't believe you know anything about fishing. Either that or there are no fish in here—one of the two."

He had turned his head toward the Bear as he spoke and was not looking at his float. All at once the Bear sat straight up, pointing at the water.

"Your cork's gone!" he shouted. "You 've got one! Pull, Bo, pull!"

The little boy turned so quickly that he almost lost his balance and could not immediately obey. Horatio was wild with excitement.

"Why don't you pull?" he howled. "Do you expect him to climb up your pole? Are you waiting for him to make his toilet before he appears? Well, talk about fishermen!"

Bosephus was struggling madly to follow instructions. He was holding to the dead limb like grim death and pulling fiercely at the pole with one hand. The fish must be a large one, for it swung furiously from side to side, but could not be brought to the surface. Horatio on the bank was still shouting and dancing violently.

"You'll lose him!" he yelled; "you'll never in the world land him that way. You ought to go fishing for tin fish in a tub! Just let me out there; I'll show you how to fish!" and Horatio made a rush toward the log on which Bo was standing.

"Go back! Go back!" screamed the little boy. "It won't hold us both!" But the Bear was too much excited by this time to heed any caution. He hurried to the centre of the log and seizing the pole from Bo's hand gave a fierce pull. The fish swung clear of the water and far out on the bank, but the strain on their support was too great. There was a loud crack-

"HORATIO ON THE BANK WAS STILL SHOUTING."

ing sound, and before they knew what had happened both were struggling in the water.

"Help! Help!" howled Horatio. "I'm drowning!"

"Hold to the end of the log!" shouted Bo. "I'll swim ashore and tow you in with the pole!"

He struck out as he spoke and in a few strokes was near enough to seize some bushes that overhung the water. Suddenly he heard Horatio give forth a scream so wild that he whirled about to look. Then he saw something that made him turn cold. In a half circle, a few feet away from where Horatio was clinging to the end of the broken log for dear life, there had risen from the water a number of long, black, ugly heads. A drove of alligators!

"Bo! Bo!" shrieked the wretched Bear. "They're after me! They'll eat me alive— skin and all! Save me! Save me!"

The little boy swung himself to the shore and dashed up the bank. His first thought had been to seize the fishing pole and with it to drag Horatio to safety. But at that instant his eye fell on the violin. He had learned to play very well himself during the last few weeks and he remembered the night of the panther dance in the Arkansaw woods. He snatched up the instrument and struck the bow across the strings.

"Sing, Horatio!" he shouted. "It's your turn to sing!" and Bosephus broke out into a song that after the first line the Bear joined as if he never expected to sing again on earth.

"Oh, there was an Old Bear went out for a swim,
And the alligators came just to take a look at him,

And the Bear was glad to see 'em, and he wanted them to stay,
And he sang a song to please 'em so they would n't go away."

"'HOLD ON TO THE END OF THE LOG!'" SHOUTED EG

THE ARKANSAW BEAR

As the music rolled out on the water there rose to the surface another half circle of dark objects. The Bear shut his eyes and his voice grew faint. They were snapping turtles.

"Stop, Bo!" he wailed. "It's no use. It only brings more of 'em, and new kinds."

"No, no; go on," whispered Bo, who had crept down quite to the water's edge. "Now—ready! sing!"

"Then 'tis 'Gator, Alligator, we expect to see you later,
If you really have to leave us—if you can't remain to tea—

Then 'tis Turtle, Mr. Turtle, you will notice we are fertile,
In providing entertainment for our com—pa—nee."

New arrivals appeared constantly until the water and logs and stumps by the water's edge were alive with listening creatures. Still remembering the panther dance the boy called in a whisper to Horatio:—

"Softly now; sing it again."

They repeated the song, letting their voices and music gradually blend into the whispering of the trees. Bo sang with closed eyes, but the watching Bear saw the listening circle of heads sink lower and lower so gently that he could not be sure when the water had closed over them. From roots and logs and stumps dark forms slid noiselessly into the stream and disappeared. The music died away and ceased. Horatio looked at the little boy eagerly.

"Quick, the pole, Bo," he called softly. "They're all gone."

A moment later he was holding on to the cane pole with teeth and claws and being towed to shore. As he marched up the bank he picked

"'SING, HORATIO! IT'S YOUR TURN TO SING!'"

up the large fish that was still flopping at the end of the line.

"Very fine, Bosephus," he said, holding it up. "You would n't have had that fish for supper if it had n't been for me, Bosephus."

THE ROAD HOME

THE ROAD HOME

CHAPTER XI

THE ROAD HOME

"Going back to Arkansaw as fast as we can go—
Never mind the winter time—never mind the
    snow,
For the weather's not so chilly as the Lou'siana
    law,
And we'll feel a good deal safer in the Ar—kan
    —saw."

IT had happened in this way. The afternoon before Christmas had come and the little boy and the Bear had been talking over a Christmas dinner for the next day.

"Bosephus," Horatio had said, "we must have something extra. I should like a real old-fashioned dinner. One such as I used to have; but, of course, that is all over now." And there was an untamed, regretful look in his eyes.

"Ratio," said Bo, "we have got a lot of money—nearly two hundred dollars. We can afford to have something good. I will buy a duck and a turkey, and maybe some pies. We'll take a holiday and eat from morning till night, if we feel like it."

The Bear smiled at this thought and touched the strings of the violin.

> " Oh, we'll buy a tender turkey, and we'll buy a youthful duck,
> And some pies, perhaps, and cookies, and some doughnuts, just for luck,
> And we'll take our Christmas dinner where the balmy breezes stray,
> And we'll spread it in the sunshine and we'll eat—all—day."

Suddenly he paused in his singing and listened. They were coming out into an open space and there was a sound of a voice speaking. Somebody was talking in a foreign language that Bo did not understand, but the Bear trembled with eagerness.

"Bo," he whispered, "that's Italian. That's the way my first teacher talked. The one that abused me—and died."

The Bear licked out his tongue fiercely at this memory and pushed forward into the open, the little boy following. As they stepped out where they could see, Bosephus uttered an exclamation and Horatio a snort of surprise. By the roadside sat a dark-browed, villainous-looking Italian, and before him stood a miserable, half-starved bear cub, which he was trying to teach. He would speak a few words to it and then beat it fiercely with a heavy stick. The little bear cowered and trembled and could not obey. Horatio gave a low, dangerous growl as Bo held him back. The Italian turned and saw them.

"What are you beating that cub for?" asked Bo, sternly.

The Italian looked at him evilly.

"Maka him grow an' dance, and playa fid, lika yo' bear," he said, sullenly. "Soa he maka da mun'."

"That won't do it. You can teach him better with kindness. Throw that stick away. Are n't you ashamed of yourself."

"Minda yo' own biz," was the insolent reply.

The little boy saw that it would not be safe to stay there any longer. The cub was whining pitifully and Horatio was becoming furious. He turned away, the Bear following reluctantly. When they had gone perhaps a half a mile Horatio paused.

"Let's camp," he said. "This is a nice place and I'm tired."

Bosephus was tired, too. The day before Christmas, with its merry preparation, had been

"'MINDA YOUR OWN BIZ.'"

a big day among the plantations, and the friends had reaped a harvest.

"All right, Ratio," he said, and they made preparations for the night, though it was still quite early.

"Bo," said the Bear, reflectively, "Christmas always reminds me of when I was a little cub like that poor little fellow we saw back yonder. I was a Christmas present—by accident."

"A Christmas present by accident! How was that?"

"It was this way. I was always brave and adventurous, as you know. My folks lived in a very large tree and were all asleep for the winter except me. I stayed awake so as to run away and see the world. Well, I started out and I traveled and I traveled. It was all woods and I lost my way. By and by I got very tired and climbed up into a thick evergreen tree to rest. I suppose I went to sleep and some men who were out hunting for a Christmas tree must have picked out mine and tied the limbs together tight with cords and cut it down. Then I suppose they must have carried me home and set the tree up in its place and untied the cords, for the first I knew I was tumbling out on to a carpet in a big room, and a lot of children were screaming and running in every direction. I was bigger and some fatter than that cub we saw with the Italian—poor little fellow!

"I'd like to talk to that villain about five minutes alone," continued Horatio, grimly. I'm sure I could interest him. I'd tell him about the man that used to beat me, and I might give him an imitation of what happened to him," and the big fellow rose and walked back and forth in excitement.

"But go on with your story, Ratio; what happened to you after you fell out of the Christmas tree?"

"Oh! the children tamed me and fed me till I got so big they were afraid of me, and then I ate up some young pigs and a calf and went away."

"You ran away, you mean. What happened then?"

"Well, I went quite a distance and fell in with a circus. I learned to dance there and stayed with them a while. But one day the young ibex came in to see me and they could n't find anything of him after that except his horns, and seemed suspicious of me, so I went away again."

"Oh, Ratio!"

"Yes; I traveled and changed about a good deal till by and by I fell in with the Italian, who promised to teach me to play the violin, and he did teach me some, as you know, but he was n't kind to me, so I—I wore mourning for him a while and went away again. Then I met up with you, and you taught me the second part of our tune, and we went into partnership and I reformed, and we 've been together ever since. We've been in some pretty close places together, Bosephus, but I've always managed to pull us through safely, and you have behaved very nobly, too, at times, Bosephus — very nobly, indeed."

"Are you sure you have reformed, Horatio!"

Horatio swung the violin to his shoulder and drew the bow across the strings. Then he sang softly : —

"Oh, there's some folks say a nigger won't steal,
But I caught one in my corn-fiel'.

And there's other folks say that a Bear will tame,
But I would n't trust him with my—"

he hesitated, and then, with a final flourish,

"with my money all the same."

THE ARKANSAW BEAR

The little boy laughed. The Bear seemed to have forgotten the cruel Italian, and was in his usual good humor.

"I think I can trust you, Horatio; I'm not a bit afraid of you."

"Bo," said Ratio, speaking suddenly, "speaking of Christmas trees, we ought to have one. I saw a beautiful one up the stream yonder. I think I'll go and get it, if you'll look after the supper while I'm gone."

"Why, yes, Horatio, only don't be long about it."

Horatio struck the violin with a long, vigorous sweep. He was very happy, and the prospect of a good dinner made him musical.

"Oh, we'll have a tree for Christmas in this Louisiana isthmus,
   Where the orange trees are waving and the jasmines are in bloom;

And I'll have a Christmas dinner, if I don't I
   am a sinner,
And I'll eat it if it sends me to my doom—
   doom—doom.'

Bo laughed again. He had never seen Horatio in a better humor.

"If you eat too much pie it may send you to your doom—doom—doom," he said. "Hurry back, now, with that tree. You can pull it up by the roots and we'll plant it again here. Then it will keep right on growing."

The Bear set out up the stream and the boy busied himself with building a fire and taking out of a sack a lot of food that had been given them by the planters during the afternoon. He spread this on the leaves and moss, and then sat down and gazed into the bright blaze. It was pleasant and warm, and he was quite tired. After a while he wondered sleepily why the

Bear did n't come back, and concluded he was having a hard time pulling up the tree. Then he began thinking of all the adventures they had had together and of the little cub bear and the cruel Italian.

"I was tempted to let Horatio at him," he thought. "A man like that should be beaten until he could n't stand. That poor little creature! How wistfully he looked at us. He kept whining—perhaps he was telling Ratio something."

The little boy's head nodded forward now and then, and presently he slept. He slept soundly and the moments flew by unheeded. He was having a long dream about old man Todd and the girls and the two candy hearts, when suddenly there arose close at hand such a commotion, such a mingling of excited language, fierce snarls, and crashing of brush that the little boy leaped to his feet wildly.

THE ARKANSAW BEAR

"Ratio!" he shouted. "Ratio! where are you?"

The only answer was the redoubled fury of the furious uproar, which Bo now located at the edge of the road but a few feet away. He tore through the brush hastily in that direction. As he reached the spot the turmoil ceased, and he heard the sound of running feet. Dashing through into the road he beheld a strange sight. A half-naked man was disappearing over the hill just beyond, and Horatio, holding some rags of clothing in one hand and the paw of the little bear in the other, was looking after him hungrily, as if about to pursue. Before him lay the Christmas tree badly broken and bruised.

"Ratio!" exclaimed Bo. "What have you been doing?"

The Bear looked at Bo sheepishly.

"I went for the Christmas tree," he said, meekly, "and just as I was coming back the Italian man came along, and he was beating this

"A HALF NAKED MAN WAS DISAPPEARING OVER THE HILL."

little chap, and so I tried the Christmas tree on him to see how he liked it. Then we got into an argument, and when he went away he left the cub with us and didn't take all of his clothing."

The little boy reflected a moment.

"I hope, Horatio," he said, gravely, "you did not mean to break your agreement about— you know—about dinners."

"I did n't, Bo; honest, I did n't. I would n't touch that fellow if I was starving. But I did pretty nearly break his neck, Bo, and I 'm glad of it!"

"Ratio," said Bo, solemnly, "it 's very wrong, I suppose; very wrong, indeed; but I'm glad, too. Only we 've got to postpone that Christmas dinner. That fellow will be back here to-night with officers, and we 've had all the law we want. We start for Arkansaw in five minutes. A bite of supper and then right about! ready! march!"

And this was the reason Horatio and Bosephus and the little cub bear were traveling swiftly northward in spite of the winter weather that was not yet over. The cub was small and weak and Horatio, who loved him and sometimes called him "litttle brother," often carried him. They gave no performances, but only pushed forward, mile after mile, chanting solemnly —

"Going back to Arkansaw as fast as we can go—
Never mind the winter time and never mind the snow,
For the weather's not so chilly as the Lou'siana law,
And we'll feel a good deal safer in the Ar—kan—saw."

"'RIGHT ABOUT! READY! MARCH!'"

THE BEAR COLONY AT LAST.
THE PARTING OF BOSEPHUS
AND HORATIO

CHAPTER XII

THE BEAR COLONY AT LAST. THE PARTING OF BOSEPHUS AND HORATIO

" Oh, the wind blows fair and the snow is gone
In the Arkansaw when the spring comes on.
Oh, the sun shines warm and the wind blows fair,
For the boy and the cub and the Old—Black Bear."

SO sang Bosephus and Horatio as they sat side by side in the doorway of a deserted lumberman's cabin in the depths of an Arkansaw forest. The cub rescued from the brutal Italian and brought with them on their hasty journey out of Louisiana stood a few feet away, watching them intently. Now and then he made an awkward attempt at dancing, which caused Bosephus and Horatio to stop their music and laugh. He had grown fat and saucy with good treatment, and seemed to enjoy the amusement he caused. At a little distance behind him, some seated and some standing, and all enjoying the entertainment, were seven other bears of various sizes. The colony so long planned by Horatio and Bosephus was formed.

The long journey out of Louisiana had been made rapidly and with no delays. Though midwinter when begun, the weather had been beautiful at the start, and there had been few storms and but little cold since. The cub had gradually told his story to Horatio, who loved him and continued to call him, affectionately, "little brother." He had been captured in a very deep woods, he said, by hunters, who sold him to the Italian. He did not know where these woods were, but as the friends crossed the Louisiana line and entered lower Arkansaw he grew more and more excited every day, for he declared these were so like his native woods that he could almost hear his mother's voice crooning the evening lullaby. Soon after they came one evening upon a deserted lumberman's camp and took possession of the one cabin that still remained. It was a good shelter and there was a stream with fine fish in it close at hand. But when the friends awoke next morning the little bear was gone.

They were very sorry, for they had grown much attached to the little chap, and he had seemed to be fond of them also. It was very lonely in the deep forest without him. Horatio sighed.

"He did n't appreciate us, Bo," he said, sadly. "He's gone back to be a wild bear. He never got the taste of men—tastes, I mean, and I suppose these woods made him homesick. They are like my old woods, too, and I get homesick sometimes—even now."

Then the boy and the Bear went to the brook to fish, and the day passed gloomily.

But that night, when Bo had built a fire in the big fireplace which almost filled one end of the cabin, and was cooking the fish, there came a muffled scratching sound at the door. Horatio sprang to his feet instantly.

"That's Cub!" he said, excitedly.

The boy ran to the door and opened it. Sure enough, the little cub stood before him, and out of the darkness behind gleamed seven other pairs of eyes. The boy was brave, but as he saw that row of fiery orbs he felt his flesh creep and his hair began to prickle.

"Horatio!" he called, softly, "come quick."

The Bear was already by his side, and a moment later, with the cub, stepped out into the night. Then Bosephus heard low growls followed by a strange commotion, which he at first took to be the sound of fighting. Suddenly Horatio ran to him in great excitement.

"Bo, Bo!" he exclaimed, "it's my family! and, oh, Bosephus, it's Cub's family, too! We're really brothers, and we did n't know it!" Then he ran back into the dark and presently returned with the cub and the seven other bears, following. The newcomers stared and blinked at the little boy as they entered the lighted cabin, and then withdrew to a darker corner, where they sat silently looking at everything that passed, like strangers from the country. The cub sat with them and whispered softly, in the bear tongue, and Horatio now and then went over, too, and no doubt told them marvelous tales of his strange adventures. Late that night all lay down to sleep—the little boy in the arms of his faithful friend.

And so the Bear Colony had begun, even sooner than Bo and Ratio had expected, and they had given up all notion of traveling any farther. The lumber camp was deserted for good by the woodcutters, for the largest trees had been cut out and taken away long before. The cabin was headquarters—Bosephus was president, Horatio prime minister, and the cub, because of his adventures and what he had already learned, was chief assistant. Early spring was upon the land, and the woods were beginning to be sweet with song and blossom. Bosephus was almost afraid at first that, with the native woods and the renewal of home ties, Horatio might return more or less to his savage instincts, but he became gentler and more docile than ever. His place as prime minister and chief instructor made him realize his advancement and the importance of good behavior. He was grave and dignified, and about the fire in the evening played the violin with an air of skill and superiority that was very impressive. Bosephus at first enjoyed it all immensely. The bears were obedient and submissive, and were gradually learning to understand his language. He had more money than

"BOSEPHUS AT FIRST ENJOYED IT IMMENSELY."

he would ever need and was lord of all he surveyed.

But gradually there came a change. He grew tired of seeing only the black faces and shining eyes of his subjects, and of hearing only the singing of bees and birds. At first he did not realize what was the matter. Then it came to him at last that this life of the forest was palling upon him and that, like the cub, he yearned for his own kind—the faces of men.

One morning he divided up the money into two equal parts and slipped out to where Horatio was sunning himself and playing softly before the cabin.

"Horatio," he said tenderly, "I have divided up the money. Here is your half. You have been the best friend I ever had and it breaks my heart to leave you, but I can't live away from my own race any longer. I am going back to Louisiana, to the planter who told me to come back and he would send me to school

THE ARKANSAW BEAR

and college and make a man of me," and then the little boy suddenly broke down and fell weeping into his companion's arms.

For some moments Horatio could not speak. Then he spoke, sobbing between every word.

"Bo—Bo—you—you 're—not going to—to leave me! Oh, Bo!" and the poor Bear gave way completely and wept on the little boy's shoulder. They were all alone, as the others had gone out together for a walk. At last Horatio put the boy gently from him and took up his violin. He began to play very softly and sang in a breaking voice :—

> "Oh, he 's going away to leave me, to the Lou'-siana shore.
> And I 'll never see my darling, my Bosephus, any more;
> He 's divided up the money, and he 's going far away,
> And my poor old heart is breaking, but he—will—not—stay.

"THE POOR BEAR WEPT ON THE LITTLE BOY'S SHOULDER."

We have battled with the weather—we have
  faced the world together—
Never caring why or whether—never minding
  when or where—
But he says we now must sever—happy days
  are done forever,
For Bosephus and the fiddle and the Old—
  Black—Bear!"

An hour later Bo was wending his way southward through the sweet spring woods alone. In his inner breast pocket was stored every dollar the friends had earned together.

"I will never need it now, Bo," Horatio had said at parting, "and you will need a great many times as much. Take it and sometimes think of your far-off, faithful Ratio." And then, after one long embrace, they had parted. And now the little boy was trying to keep up courage to carry out what he had undertaken. At every turn in the path he was tempted to return and throw himself in Horatio's arms. But he pressed on, hoping to arrive at some sort of

THE ARKANSAW BEAR

habitation for the night, which he did not like to pass alone in the woods.

"Poor old Ratio," he thought. "He will be happier with his own people after a while. And perhaps he will really civilize them." He turned and cast one long look in the direction of the colony, which he could no longer see. Then facing about again he hurried forward. About a mile further on he paused at a little brook for a drink. He was bending over the water when he heard a sudden crashing in the bushes behind him. He started up instantly and seized a heavy stick that lay close at hand. Nearer and nearer came the tearing through the brush, like some heavy animal in fierce chase. The boy stepped out of the path to let the creature pass, and then, all at once, he gave a cry of joy and surprise. Headlong out of the bushes, stumbling and rolling at his feet, with tears streaming from his eyes and violin under his arm, was Horatio.

"Bo, Bo!" he cried. "I'm going with you. That kind planter will give me a place to stay, I know, and maybe if he sends you to college he'll let me go, too. I could play for the college boys, Bo, and help pay your way. Don't send me back, Bo!"

Bo embraced him silently.

"Why, of course not, Ratio," he said at last, "but I thought you wanted to have a colony."

"I did, Bo, but I have turned it over to Cub. He can take care of it. Like you, Bo, I have been civilized too long to live away from men! And, besides, Bo, you need me to protect you." Horatio recovered his dignity at this point and continued, gravely, "You are brave and noble, Bosephus, but you need some one near you who is ever ready to face any danger. Let us sing now, Bosephus, as we travel onward."

And with a joyful scrape of the strings and a sweet burst of melody the friends set their faces once more to the South.

THE ARKANSAW BEAR

"Oh, there was a little boy and his name was Bo,
Went out into the woods when the moon was low,

And he met an Old Bear who was hungry for a snack,
And the folks are still awaiting for Bosephus to come back.

For the boy became the teacher of this kind and gentle creature,
Who was faithful in his friendship and was watchful in his care.

And they traveled on forever and they'll never, never sever,
Bosephus and the fiddle and the Old—Black—Bear."

"And they traveled on forever"

Publisher's Note—What happened to Bosephus, with the further Adventures of Horatio, are told in "Elsie and the Arkansaw Bear."